THE HEREAFTER

Matthew Sandage

The Hereafter
Copyright © 2022 Matthew Sandage

Produced and printed by Stillwater River Publications.
All rights reserved. Written and produced in the
United States of America. This book may not be reproduced
or sold in any form without the expressed, written
permission of the author and publisher.

Visit our website at
www.StillwaterPress.com
for more information.

First Stillwater River Publications Edition

ISBN: 978-1-955123-79-2

1 2 3 4 5 6 7 8 9 10

Written by Matthew Sandage
Cover artwork by Tithi Luadthong & Matthew St. Jean
Cover & interior book design by Matthew St. Jean
Published by Stillwater River Publications,
Pawtucket, RI, USA.

*The views and opinions expressed
in this book are solely those of the author
and do not necessarily reflect the views
and opinions of the publisher.*

For my beautiful Blue Jay.

*Thank you to all of those who have
supported me throughout this endeavor
as well as my life in general.*

*I also like to thank you, Steven;
you've given me what I needed
all along... a chance.*

PART I

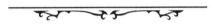

WHISPERS OF THE HEREAFTER

In a dreary world filled with vibrant flashes of light, malevolent and malformed creatures, as well as freakish flora, a young man treads like an incurable moose through muddy waters, being lured by some unforeseeable force. With each step, the purplish-pink translucent ground beneath his bare feet glows like a flickering candle then changes to blood-red. The air flowing about him is thick and burdensome like a noxious fume and smells of sulfur. Blue and green lightning strikes skip along the surface of the hurricane clouds circling above. In its center is a black gaping hole leading to a place very few travelers wish to go.

When the young man is nearly two miles away from the center of the cosmic cyclone, he maneuvers past an arrangement of jagged obsidian rocks, appearing like the bottom row of a shark's set of teeth. Atop the cryptic crags, a group of tiny beings resembling the mix between a goblin and fury congregate, cheer, and chant. Although the language is well beyond the young man's familiarity, he can make out one word that's repeated on several occasions: "Ka-Throm... Ka-Throm... Ka-Throm..." As the crowd of curious creatures continue their cheering and chanting, the young man treads forward with what feels like eels in the pit of his stomach.

Eventually, the cheering and chanting grows silent as they are soon overpowered by a throng of blue, translucent trees of some sort singing a chilling hymn—a hymn taking the form of a chorus of screeching sopranos. Through the trees' crystal bark, the young man can see what lies ahead. Before long, he emerges from the unimaginable forest and stands before *it*.

Miles beneath the eye of the unnerving hurricane is another gaping hole, a hole much wider than the one above. As soon as the young man arrives at the edge of the abyss, the now distant translucent trees simultaneously cease their song as if being hushed by the composer. From the abyss rises the most disturbing beast the young man has ever seen.

Rising before the young man is a massive creature bearing a red, fleshy, bony body. Its lower half resembles a serpent. It's upper is muscular and open, exposing torn muscle, a cracked rib cage, and at its center, a black beating heart. It's six arms are also muscular with portions of the skin peeled back. Over the course of its entire body, the creature is speckled with puss-squirting blisters. Its head looks similar to a basilisk's with Medusa hair. From its back emerges a set of eight spindly crustacean legs. The young man takes one look, then shields his eyes with his hands.

"Vrak-na-kar, Ka-Throm. Voon-na-tar, Erdronta!" the being roars in a demonic, hissing voice. But the young man still doesn't turn.

As a result of the young man's behavior, the being shouts at him, expelling a gust of air from its mouth that almost topples him. It repeats itself once more. This time, the foreign language becomes familiar.

"Vrak-na-kar, Ka-Throm. Voon-na-tar, Erdronta! My name is Ka-Throm. And this is the Hereafter!"

Once the young man is able to determine the arcane articulation, he unshields his eyes and stares up into the being's peculiar pair. Although its body is beyond comprehension, its eyes are human but glassy like a doll's eyes. Suddenly, the being lifts its arms toward the thunderous sky, causing the purplish-pink and red earth to shake beneath the young man's feet. Then, it opens its mouth like a squid, releasing a harmonious hum, and a swarm of winged things gather above.

While watching the outlandish phenomenon take place, the young man feels something like a raindrop hit his exposed right shoulder blade. He picks up the red droplet on his shoulder with his left pointer finger and presses it to his tongue. The droplet is warm and instantly tastes like iron. Just as the young man realizes what's about to happen, a shower of blood rains down from the sky. As the young man attempts to flee from the unidentifiable being and the abyss before him, his white tank top is tie-dyed and his black pajamas become soaked. Worst of all, the being perceives his efforts.

With another lift of its hands, the earth surrounding the young man begins to quake, erode, and crumble. The man's heart is jolting as fast as humanly possible and feels as if someone or something is stabbing it with a knife. But the young man's efforts to flee are futile as the earth opens beneath him and he falls for what seems like an eternity.

That is, until he lands on his bed, wriggling atop his sweat-stained sheets. The young man rampantly wakes from his nightmare and is never the same again.

PART II

MIRRORING WORLDS

I.

On the second floor of a presumably abandoned apartment complex called Tombstone Temple, and in a room located at the end of a hallway with the numbers "237" barely clinging to the crimson red doorway, is a group of forensic scientists, police officials, as well as detectives gathering around a peculiar black cult symbol chalked into the weathered floorboards. In the middle of the symbol, resembling a mind-numbing mandala, is a stripped young woman with her heart ripped out. Her chest cavity is completely exposed, and the torn flesh around the unpleasant extraction has become the petals of an orange gerbera.

The two detectives at the crime scene are partners Ken Connelly and Dexter Williams. Ken is a fair-skinned and rather slim young man while Dexter is dark-skinned and vigorous. This is the third time within the past month Ken and Dexter have happened upon a cult crime scene, and each supposed sacrifice mimics the last. Even after conducting extensive research, a dozen walkthroughs, multiple fingerprint sweeps, as well as identifying and collecting possible evidence, they have yet to gain a lead regarding the ongoing investigation. But tonight will change everything.

While Dexter speaks with Sergeant Blackwood on the phone and receives his fill of "cellular chastisement for the day," as he calls it, Ken maneuvers between an overlapping circle of candles, trying his best not to catch his suit pants on fire. After maneuvering through the candlelit maze, he eventually arrives at a tilted cracked mirror on the wall. As he stares at his own slim features in the reflection, he begins to hear something chanting through the crack and puts his right ear up against the cold glass. The words echo clearly in a soft, feminine voice: "Ka-Throm… Ka-Throm... Ka-Throm…" But the chanting ceases once Dexter finishes his phone call and beckons Ken.

"What in God's name do ya think you're doin'?" Dexter says.

"Nothing… nothing at all, Dex," Ken says and backs away from the mirror.

"Well, stop actin' crazy and get ya ass over here!"

Ken maneuvers through the candles once more and stands beside his partner.

"What's going on, bud?"

"Well, I just got off the phone wit' Blackwood and she's about to tear us a new one."

Dexter and Ken turn toward the coroner who has come to collect the body. He wraps the young woman up in a white cloth and drives her out of the room on a stretcher.

"Perfect, just what we need. I mean, I don't understand why we have yet to collect any evidence that gives us at least one suspect. We've swept for fingerprints, conducted extensive research..."

"I don't know, man. Maybe we need a new angle."

"What do you mean, Dex?"

"Ya know, a new way of looking at things."

"Maybe. Hopefully the toxicology report will tell us something."

"I don't know, let's just check the place out tomorrow in the daylight. Place is givin' me the creeps."

"I'm hearing you on that one!"

"Can I make the call?"

"Yes, it's your turn, my man."

"Alright, hey everyone! Clear out! We can regroup in the mornin' and double check to see if we missed somethin'! Have a goodnight!"

As the forensic scientists, police officials, and detectives pack up their things, extinguish the candles, and vacate the premises, Ken can still hear the distant chant of something sinister and yet oddly alluring in the back of his mind.

"Ka-Throm... Ka-Throm... Ka-Throm..."

II.

At about four in the morning, the door labeled "237" opens and Ken creeps around the door like a devious thief. After entering and shutting the door behind him, he crosses over the black symbol and stands before the mirror a second time. At first, no sound echoes from beyond or within the fractured glass frame. But then, Ken hears another voice coming from the crack, something ominous and different from before. Something more demonic and malevolent. He places his right ear to the cold crack and listens.

"Vrak-na-kar, Ka-Throm. Voon-na-tar, Erdronta!"

Ken pulls away from the mirror, giving it a look of bewilderment, then places his ear to the crack again.

"My name is Ka-Throm. And this is the Hereafter!"

After the voice speaks clearly in English, he feels something warm and slippery slither into his ear. Ken attempts to pull his head away from the mirror, but he can't. The slippery, slimy appendage is now deep; so deep in fact that it pierces his eardrum and bursts it like a water balloon. Once the eardrum bursts, the foul appendage retracts out of Ken's ear and back into the mirror's crack.

"I can't... I can't hear!" Ken screams and presses his right palm to his right earlobe and uses it as a plunger.

Once he pulls his hand away from his earlobe and looks at it, he instantly sees and feels a pool of lukewarm blood. His hand shakes and the blood jolts from his hand like water from a sprinkler. After staring at his blood sprinkling the floorboards beneath his back dress shoes, he hears the voice again. Only this time, it sounds as if the voice is speaking through a megaphone.

"My name is Ka-Throm. And this is the Hereafter!"

A tenacious gust of wind bursts from the mirror's crack, though it doesn't cause Ken to capsize, and this is because he has become immobilized like an evergreen in a wintery windstorm.

"What's happening? Why can't I feel my—"

Before Ken can finish his sentence, he sees some *thing* in the mirror. The thing staring back at him is no longer his reflection, or is it? He places his right hand, no, his right tentacle to his wrinkly, withering face and touches his third eye now growing from a fleshy stem in the center of his forehead.

"WHAT IS HAPPENINGGGG?"

As his own voice becomes unrecognizable, he removes the .40 caliber semi-automatic Smith & Wesson pistol from his holster and places its chamber to his right temple.

"Forg…ive…me…Dex."

Ken pulls the trigger, and his head combusts like a missile in mid-air, spraying the room in shimmering, teal-colored blood.

III.

The next day, Dexter arrives back at room "237" with his colleagues to see if they can uncover something, anything to give them direction in the cases of the three young women, including Susan Davenport, Holly Graves, and now, Emma Summers. They all wait a few minutes outside the room for Ken to arrive. After a while, they begin to assume he's probably still sleeping and enter the room anyways. What they find behind room "237" on October 22nd, 2021 is unimaginable and indescribable. They will never be the same again.

PART III

DOG GONE DEAD

Sifting through the overgrown grass of Mr. Lennon's backyard with her snout is a gorgeous golden retriever named Sally. As she circles around the yard, sniffing the night air, grass spears, odorous wildflowers, and the soil's stinging aroma of ammonia, she discovers a gaping hole beside a forgotten garden. Curious, as most creatures are, she uses her snout and night vision to inspect the gaping hole and is instantly entranced by its depth, groups of kaleidoscope-colored crystals lining its inside, and a vibrant, brilliant light at the end of the transcendental tunnel.

As she continues to glare in the hole, its beguiling quality slowly shifts to sinister as something emerges from the brilliant light: a spider-like creature with ten legs, a plump, spherical body, a head resembling a hyena's, and a scorpion stinger dripping with a purple secretion. As the creature steps closer to Sally, while making a chilling clicking noise with its forked tongue, she begins to bark and whimper in an effort to warn her owner.

Eventually, Mr. Lennon hears Sally's cries over the sounds of his blaring TV, prompting him to pause the Patriots vs. the Green Bay Packers game and exit his house through the back door. When he arrives on the decaying floorboards of his back porch, he scans the yard for Sally. Although he can hear Sally panting and barking, he struggles to locate her as a result of the forest growing from his savage lawn.

"What's wrong, girl? What is it?"

Sally responds the only way she can, and Mr. Lennon begins to feel as though there are worms wiggling their way through his intestines.

"Alright, girl! Let me grab my gun! Just hold on one second, I'll be right back!"

Mr. Lennon goes back inside his house and returns holding his 12-gauge shotgun.

"Alright, girl! I'm coming!"

Mr. Lennon snakes through the tall grass carefully, like a drunk driver taking a sobriety test, holding his shotgun above his head. As he makes his way toward Sally, her barks and whimpers suddenly stop. Then he hears a single, ear-piercing yelp.

"Sally! Are you alright, girl?"

Mr. Lennon's pace quickens, but suddenly slows down and comes to a complete stop just before reaching Sally. She's beginning to make noises again, though this time, they resemble a mixture between the howling of a wolf and the hysterical laughs of a pack of hyenas. As he inches closer, he begins to see Sally's body jolting as if being shocked by a defibrillator, growing as well as changing.

"Sally? You okay, girl? C'mon, there's no need to hide. I'm here now, and everything's going to be alright. I'm not going to let anything hurt—"

Before Mr. Lennon can finish his sentence, Sally's body rises from the tall grass, towering over it and her owner. As soon as her body ceases to rise and remains idle, he begins to make out her new physical appearance. From her chest down to where her hind legs used to be now mimic the body of a snake, her front legs have taken on the appearance of a T-Rex's, and she now bears three hairless and fleshless heads. While staring at Mr. Lennon with her white eyes, Sally's trio of heads simultaneously writhe, moan, and make a clicking sound with their forked tongues. After a few minutes of moaning and clicking, her sounds change to a woman's voice, a woman who sounds as if she's being mutilated.

"Plays! Kell! May!"

"What has happened to my girl? What have they done to you?"

Mr. Lennon sheds a couple of tears, then quickly wipes them away with one of the white armholes of his tank top.

"I don't want to... but I must. Goodbye, my sweet, playful girl. Forgive me, Charlotte."

He raises his shotgun and aims it at Sally's throng of heads. She repeats herself once more.

"Plays! Kell!..."

Before saying "May," Mr. Lennon blasts her faces away with three shots of his gun. Because he lives rather close to his neighbors, the booms of the blasts disturb their sleep and provoke them to call the police. Some of those who are brave enough to venture to Mr. Lennon's backyard to check to see if he's safe arrive before the first responders and happen upon the unspeakable turmoil: a contorted corpse of a dog as well as a scarred man with a teal-colored, blood-stained tank top. Shortly after Sally's disturbing departure from this world, the hole that started the whole plight disappears.

PART IV

A TRAIL OF STOLEN HEARTS

I.

Shortly after witnessing the mangled, deformed body of his partner Ken Connelly in room "237" of the abandoned Tombstone Temple apartment complex, Detective Dexter Williams locates a hidden grimoire tucked away behind the wall of the room's only closet. He notices the mandala symbol chalked on the floor is the same exact one etched into the book's front cover and opens it to about halfway. *Whoosh*! A small gust of air, smelling of a noxious belch, smacks Dexter in the face like a metal bat. After wafting away the smell, he notices the language scribbled on each flimsy page is not recognizable. So much so he hardly believes an astute linguist could interpret the haunting array of hieroglyphs. To avoid allowing the book to be seen by his fellow colleagues, he quickly shuts it and conceals it by placing it underneath the back side of his navy-blue dress shirt as well as his black suit jacket. Dexter doesn't look at the grimoire again until later that night when he's alone in his house.

Hours pass and he finally has a chance to look at the grimoire beneath the intimate light of a small desk lamp in his study. As he flips through the pages, tracing each hieroglyph with his long, slender fingers, he happens upon a page that is recognizable: a map.

The detailed map labeled "Appalachian Trail" shows a trail leading through a thick forest atop a windy mountain pass, but instead of an "X" marking the spot, it's a heart. After seeing the heart, everything in Dexter's mind begins to click like a silver ball bearing hitting all the hot spots in a pinball machine. The cult, the extracted hearts, and the grimoire all connect, but it doesn't make Dexter feel at ease. It only brings him more pain as he recalls his best friend's body lying limp on the frosty floor, dead, alone, and with no answer as to how he ended up the way he did, except for a brief, perplexing message written in teal blood on the moldy wall beside his body, which read, "The Hereafter." This sudden recollection of his best friend causes a cauldron of molten madness to begin brewing inside, driving him to immediately pack up a few things, leave his home in the middle of the night, and follow the trail of stolen hearts leading to Ken's killers.

II.

After about a two-hour drive from eastern to western Connecticut, Dexter finds a place to park his car and enter along the trail. The parking lot is nearly empty except for a few cars parked in front of a mini mart titled "Miny's Mini-Mart." Once he finishes unpacking his hiking gear from the trunk of his car, he decides to stop inside Miny's and ask the manager if he has seen any curious customers lately, as well as to grab some food and water supplies. After entering the store, moseying up and down the aisles, and grabbing everything he needs for his journey, he stands behind a young man who's also waiting to check out. Dexter eyes the man's body like a nosey child and realizes he has no gear, nor is he wearing appropriate hiking attire.

"Hey, young man, I hope ya not thinkin' of hikin' that trail wearin' that."

The young man turns around and squints his eyes at him. "Why don't you mind your own business, old man!"

"What did ya call me?"

The young man's face shifts from disgust to shame. "I'm...I'm sorry. I just...I haven't had much sleep lately."

"Bad dreams?"

"Nightmares are more like it."

"Sorry, I hate that shit. Sleep is one of the betta ways of replenishin' our bodies... Hell, I haven't had much sleep lately either. But hey, how about we start ova. My name's Dexter Williams, what's yours?"

Dexter reaches out a hand to shake with the young man's, nearly dropping the food and water he has pressed to his chest.

"The name's Victor Emberton."

"Cool name, kid. So, tell me, Victor, what brings ya to the Appalachian Trail? Like I said before, ya lookin' a little unda prepared."

Victor looks down at himself, then back at Dexter. "The Hereafter."

"The what?"

"A week ago, I had this dream…"

As Victor and Dexter continue to speak to one another, the color of the cashier's face changes from off-white to scarlet red.

"Alright, are you two going to buy something, or just continue to waste my time?"

Victor and Dexter respond simultaneously.

"Sorry about that."

The two move aside to let another customer cut in front of them.

"As I was saying, I had this dream, well, nightmare about a week ago…" Victor continues once the customer passes by.

"The Hereafter! Ya know what it is?"

"Yes, wait… you've heard of it before?"

Digging up the recent past pierces Dexter in the gut.

"Yea, my best friend, my partner... honestly, I'm not really sure what happened. I just know that I found him dead on the floor of a nasty apartment wit' his head blown off, and his body... his body was different. Like somethin' out of John Carpenter's *The Thing*...and there was this message on the wall, I can only assume was written by my friend before he died, and it said 'The Hereafter.' But how do you know about it? And ya can tell me this time, I promise not to interrupt ya."

Victor takes a moment to stare at Dexter in shock, then resume the conversation.

"I had a nightmare a week ago that felt so real. I was walking in, like, another dimension or something, filled with vibrant colors, horrifying creatures, and a towering monster that's, needless to say, difficult to describe in words. The monster told me its name was Ka-Throm and the place we were in was called The Hereafter. As soon as I woke up from the nightmare, I had this freakish feeling like I was meant to be somewhere and that feeling led me here. I didn't pack my things, I just left."

For a moment, the two stand in silence.

"Look, I know this sounds crazy, but you got to believe me..."

"I do."

"This might sound insane as well, but I think I was meant to find you. I just have yet to learn why."

"I think I know."

Dexter places all of the food and water down onto the white and black tiled floor, then reaches into his blue backpack and removes the grimoire with the black mandala symbol etched into its cover. Before showing it to Victor, he takes a moment to caress the symbol.

"Within this here book lies the key to unlockin' the meanin' of your dreams and the answer as to who killed my friend. I can't read the damn thing, but there's a map..."

"A map? Let me see."

Victor stands beside Dexter as he opens the book to the first page. Victor reads the first line aloud.

"'Lend your heart and reap the reward of a world falling apart.'"

"Wait? You can read this?"

"Yes? Can't you? It's written in English."

Dexter stares at Victor in disbelief.

"No, it's not."

Without warning, Victor rips the book from Dexter's hands like an impatient beggar, storms over to the cashier, and shoves it in his face.

"Can you read this?"

"What? No? It looks like some made-up fantasy language. No one could read that shit."

"Thank you... er..." Victor attempts to read the man's name tag. "Johnathen!"

"No problem."

Victor returns to Dexter's side and begins to flip through the pages.

"What are ya lookin' for, kid?"

"Something, anything on Ka-Throm... Ah-hah! Here's something!" Victor quickly and softly reads each word aloud, barely loud enough for Dexter to hear. Then he suddenly stops reading and backs his face away from the grimoire.

"What? What is it!"

"We need to leave. Right. Now!"

Krack-thoom! Lightning strikes just outside Miny's, and Victor is seen rushing outside shortly after. Dexter closes the grimoire, forces it into his backpack, picks up the supplies on the floor, and begins to run out the door.

"Hey! Hey, sir! You need to pay for that!"

Dexter stops in his tracks like a scared squirrel crossing a busy street, then throws the supplies onto the countertop in front of the cashier.

"Ummm... just hold that for a second."

Dexter dashes out of the mini-mart as speedy as a person on roller-skates.

"Yeah... sure, sure, let me just hold onto this stuff for you... jackass..."

Just outside Miny's Mini-Mart, Dexter nearly bumps into Victor who's standing only a couple of feet from the door.

"Hey! What's going on—"

Before finishing his sentence, Dexter follows Victor's gaze toward a hurricane storm brewing barely above the tips of the pines a little way beyond the

Appalachian Trail's entrance. Storms are nothing new to New Englanders, but this storm is unlike anything Dexter has seen before. The clouds circling above the pines are tinged red and purple and the lightning strikes skipping along each cloud's surface like flying fish are hued lemon-yellow. A foul smell of sulfur and sewage fills the air and echoing louder than the thunder itself is a distant chant. As the storm rages, Dexter feels as though he's being put under a warlock's spell, pulling him toward the storm. Without warning, Victor places a hand on his left shoulder.

"Hey! You alright?"

"Wha... yeah, I'm good. I'm just not sure I have the strength to..."

Victor pats the distraught detective's back.

"Look, neither do I... But we can't just stand here and do nothing. A wise man once said, 'It's the action, not the fruit of the action, that's important. You have to do the right thing. It may not be in your power, may not be in your time, that there'll be any fruit. But that doesn't mean you stop doing the right thing. You may never know what results come from your action. But if you do nothing, there will be no result.'"

"Gandhi, right?"

"Yes, and he's right. If we do nothing, nothing will change for the better."

"True, but we must bear in mind change is inevitable, whether good or bad."

"Exactly! So, let's not see if we can change the fate of the world by stopping something, whatever Ka-Throm is, from entering this world."

"I like the way ya think, kid."

"Good! So, are we going to stand here and keep talking or are we actually doing something?"

"I say we go for it, and let's do it for Ken, my... my partner..."

"Let's!"

Dexter and Victor begin their journey toward the cosmic, swirling storm in the sky and the echoes of a cult who've remained like apparitions in the shadows for decades. But shortly after their arrival, they will discover some things are meant to be and the world will never be the same.

PART V

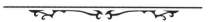

THE ENSUING OF AN EERIE END

Miles above the bustling city of Hartford, Connecticut, a group of corrupt clouds gather and circle around a mysterious, rainbow-colored hole. In addition to the stench of air pollution, a noxious fume smelling of sulfur becomes apparent. Most of the city's citizens located miles below the ensuing storm remain oblivious to what's occurring above, their gazes frozen to the light glowing from their cellular screens. But some look up and howl in horror like dogs trapped in a kennel. This soon gains the attention of everyone who is originally unaware. Even a couple cars create traffic jams in order to ascertain the situation.

Quickly drifting near the hole is an airplane, unprepared to change its course. As it soars beneath the hole, a large red and black tentacle reaches forth from the aerial abyss, grappling the airplane's nose and shaking it like a ferocious toddler. Eventually, the tentacle releases it, and the airplane becomes a meteor quickly spiraling toward one of the city's many skyscrapers. After piercing the side of a building, creating a massive cloud of smoke and fire, Hartford's citizens panic and turn into terrified ants who flee from their recently trampled anthill.

Soon, the architect of the anarchy shows itself. An enormous red and black creature with an upper body nearly identical to a bony human's and the lower of an octopus propels itself through the portal. Aside from its physical features that are similar to a human's, its head is shaped like a mutated insect with a pair of immense antennae. After displaying itself to the entire city, it raises its arms to the turbulent cyclone above, opens its mouth, and begins to speak an unrecognizable language.

"Vrak-na-kar, Ka-Throm. Voon-na-tar, Erdronta!"

This strange hymn causes everyone below to cease their disarray. They become a municipality of entranced mannequins. They even begin to hum the hymn along with the guttural sounds being produced by the creature. But the calm stops once the creature ceases its song and a horde of winged things rapidly burst from the portal, followed by beings of all colors, shapes, and sizes.

The people of Hartford, Connecticut resume their mass hysteria, the creatures flood the streets, feasting, altering, metamorphosing… and the city will never be the same again.

PART VI

DANDELION EYES

As Jasper snuggles atop a pile of clothes neatly stacked on a black dresser, positioned below a Trinity College Graduate poster and sitting beside a convulsing bed, she watches her owner, Ms. Bloom, get pounded like a printing press by the second stranger this week, and it's only Monday. Through her glowing dandelion eyes, she watches as the muscular man riding atop Ms. Bloom oozes sweat and plunges his tongue deep into her throat. In addition to the sounds of the headboard smacking against the wall, the Black-Eyed Peas' "My Humps" is blasting from a speaker phone. Amidst the noise, Jasper can still hear the voices of Ms. Bloom and her recent conquest.

"You like that? Huh, you like that?" the man says.

Eventually, after being given a chance to breathe, Ms. Bloom responds in an unenthusiastic manner.

"Oh, yeah! I love it! Give it to me, give it to me!"

As the bed rocks like a rowboat stuck in the middle

of a fierce current, an explosion echoes just outside the shaded bedroom window. This causes Jasper to rise, then resume her original position.

"What was that?"

"Ugh, I don't know… probably just a car door… ungh, from the garage. You know… how loud it can be… Can you go… ungh… on top?"

Ms. Bloom shakes off the disturbance, mounts the man, then moves her hips backwards and forward.

"Oh, yeah… I'm getting close…"

Something Ms. Bloom and her conquest lack in common. Suddenly, another explosion is heard, followed by a startled scream. She stops riding the man and points out the situation happening outside again.

"Okay, I definitely heard something."

"C'mon, babe! Let me at least finish, then we'll check it out. I'm really close, I promise."

Although Ms. Bloom is hardly being stimulated, she decides to finish the man off anyways.

"Okay but make it quick." She bends down and gives him a kiss before amping up the speed of her movements.

"Oh, yeah! Just like… ungh… that!"

As Ms. Bloom inches her conquest closer to climax, a bizarre beam of multi-colored light bursts through an opening of the shades. The light is barely noticeable to the sexual fiends, but it catches Jasper's eyes.

"Ahhhhhhhhh!"

"There you go, baby…"

When Ms. Bloom looks down at her conquest again after staring up at the ceiling and pulling her long curly hair for the past couple of minutes, she realizes the yell is not of joy, but of fear.

"Mmmmmmm!"

"What's wrong, what's wrong?"

It takes a second before Ms. Bloom realizes what's happening, but then she notices the man's lips are glued together and it appears as if he's biting down on them.

"Oh my God! Oh maaaaaaaaaaaaayyyyyyyyyy!"

From atop a pile of clothes, Jasper watches as Ms. Bloom and her conquest's bodies begin to slowly melt like a pair of humid ice sculptures into one. Their flesh and muscles torn and sticking to one another like wads of used bubblegum. Among their blending features, the most disturbing is their meshed faces. Their mouth appears to have a hair lip and their eyes are bulging from their sockets, ready to pop out at any second.

As the transformation continues to take place, Jasper's glare doesn't drift. Instead, she appears to sink deeper into the pile of clothes as her owner changes into something indistinguishable.

PART VII

THE INEVITABLE

After trudging through a couple miles of muddy hills, dodging incoming branches and meandering through a maze of fallen trees, the dynamic duo, Dexter and Victor, finally arrive at a clearing. Above the clearing is the center of the raging storm, and below is a group of at least five people dressed in black and red silk cloaks, circling around a gaping hole in the ground. With each of the cultist's arms raised toward the eye of the storm, they chant something in another language, something only Victor can understand.

While staring at the madness taking place and at the bewitched cultists, one of the people in the cloaks shift their gaze toward the duo, causing them to take cover behind a collapsed tree trunk.

"Do ya think they saw us?"

"No…" Victor peeps his head above the tree trunk and looks at the cultist whose gaze returns to the storm. "No, I think we're good!"

"Phew, this is some crazy shit!"

"You think?"

Soon, both of their phones begin to frantically beep like a pair of winning lottery machines. They quickly take the phones out of their pockets and read the alerts. In a developing news story, portals are opening along the East Coast, releasing an otherworldly Hell. The story states people must remain indoors and board up their windows in order to avoid being eaten by atrocious creatures or being transformed into one.

"What the hell is goin on, Victor?"

"I think the cult is beckoning Ka-Throm, and The Hereafter is seeping into our world!"

"Well, fuck me!"

"RRRRROOOOOOOAAAAAARRRRR!"

After hearing the loud howl and feeling the rumbling of the soil beneath their feet, Dexter and Victor both tuck their phones back into their pockets and peep their heads above the tree trunk to see what's happening.

From the storm's center, a vibrant light beams into the gaping hole below, and from the hole rises Ka-Throm like a corpse rising from a grave.

"Holy shit! We're too late, Victor!"

"We're never too late, we still have time to close the portal and stop Ka-Throm once and for all!"

"But how?"

"Is there something in that grimoire that could help us out?"

"The fuck if I'd know! I can't read it and ya know I can't!"

"Fine, give it here!"

Dexter sifts through his backpack, removes the book, then tosses it to Victor. After catching it, Victor quickly skims the book till he finds something that may be of use.

"Ah-hah! We're in luck, buddy!"

"I hope so! So, what do we do?"

"You need to stop the cultists while I take out Ka-Throm!"

"Okay, but how?"

"Just trust me on this one!"

"Trust you? Why can't ya tell me—"

Before allowing Dexter to finish his sentence, Victor runs out from behind the trunk and toward the crater of carnage.

"Shit!"

To allow Victor to get close enough to Ka-Throm, Dexter whips out his handgun and begins to shoot at each of the five cultists. His impeccable aim allows him to headshot all but one, the one standing on the opposite side of Ka-Throm. As the last cultist circles around toward the front of Ka-Throm, Victor begins to chant a phrase from the grimoire.

"Vay-thra, Ka-Throm! Vay-thra, Erdronta!"

While chanting the foreign language, Dexter takes a couple shots at the remaining cultist and misses. With a single flick of the wrist, the cultist snaps Dexter's hand backwards, causing him to drop his handgun.

"Shit, shit, shit! Victor, ya have to get outta there!"

Victor fails to hear Dexter's warning above the sounds of the swirling storm as well as the howls of Ka-Throm.

"Vay-thra, Ka-Throm! Vay-thra… uck… uck…"

"No!"

Before reading the final word in the spell, Ka-Throm pierces Victor through the chest with one of its elongated ebony nails. Blood spurts from Victor's mouth like water from a defective watering fountain.

"No, Victor!"

The sound of Ka-Throm's laughter outweighs the cries of Dexter. While the creature from beyond continues to laugh, the remaining cultist shifts its focus toward Ka-Throm and begins to bow. After taking a moment to admire the cultists' subservience, Ka-Throm raises its hands to the storm and opens its mouth. But instead of unleashing a horde of winged things, a small red and black orb drifts from within. Once leaving Ka-Throm's mouth, the orb begins to convulse then explodes, showering the neighboring area in a prism light.

This single orb of light is powerful enough to not only terraform the land surrounding it, but also to transform everyone and everything. As the light nearly blinds Dexter's vision, he watches as the body of his new friend slowly becomes an ethereal group of flowers. The sight could almost be described as something splendid. After watching his friend transform, he looks down at his own body as his limbs become the appendages of a squid and his chest grows a couple rows of spikes. As his eyes change, his sight fades from crystal clear to sky blue and he speaks one more phrase before his vocal cords renew.

"Change... is... inevi... table..."

ABOUT THE AUTHOR

MATTHEW SANDAGE is a horror writer who hails from the small town of Plainfield, Connecticut. When he's not writing ghastly tales filled with gore, suspense, and fear, he enjoys spending time with family and friends, watching movies and television shows, playing video games, as well as going on nature walks. His educational background includes attending Quinebaug Valley Community College and receiving an Associate's Degree in Pathways to Teaching Careers, attending Eastern Connecticut State University to receive his Bachelor's Degree in English, and he's currently attending Southern New Hampshire University online to gain a Master's Degree in English and Creative Writing.

Made in the USA
Middletown, DE
07 September 2022

72252516R00024